Fire Bringer

By

Eden Van Leeuwen

NATIONAL
LIBRARY
OF AUSTRALIA

A catalogue record for this
work is available from the
National Library of Australia

ISBN-13: 978-0-6450759-0-8

Cover design by: Eden Van Leeuwen.

Printed and bound by IngramSpark,
76 Discovery Road, Dandenong South Vic 3175,
Australia.

Preface

This book is a collection of short stories that have been written over a small lifetime and were finally organised into this volume in 2020.

Acknowledgments

This book is dedicated to my proofreaders, to a wonderful friend, and to my family who made this book possible by offering me their support and time.

Table of Contents

Wise Words

The din of a hundred pens tapping ensnares Wise's ears and draws her away from the computer screen to the awakened fax machine. The message unfurls from its plastic maw. Swiping up the warm paper, her eyes bound through the script.

Wise cradles the paper close. She traces the words with her fingers; the familiar hurried loops and lively scrawl hold her captive in its harsh short cursive jaws.

She crumples the cold paper in her hands, and it falls out of her grasp; she staggers out of the tiny solitary lab and up the stairs into the heart of her house. She excavates her backpack from her closet and packs listlessly.

Trampling down the stairs, at the threshold of her door, she dons a mask and gloves and heads into the dying day.

By the constellations guide, she drives past desolate cities where the dead litter the streets: to farms full of refugees who dot the landscape; to rows of trees that bear rotting fruit. She changes gloves and masks religiously. Only when no other humans are in sight does she stop this ritual.

Abandoning the car she travels by foot through fertile landscape that transmutes into a dry sea of sand and igneous rocks. Shrubs struggle up through the sandy grains that lay a path to a single tree, which flourishes on the dark cold desert plain, and a single ghost apple drips from a branch. A warm smile grazes her face; her parched throat aches in relief.

On shaky legs she walks underneath the branch; the translucent fruit hangs, tantalising, just out of reach. Wise meanders to the trunk; her long grungy nails dig into the bark and she drags herself up onto the stubby branches, snatching the apple.

She drops onto the sand and bites into the cold sweet innards, eating to the very core. Putting the remains in her coat pocket, she waits under the tree.

In the dwindling night, a fluid figure trembles into her view. A blob of water moves consciously across the ground; silver globes float in the middle of its form, giving it a childish face. Her mind whirrs as she deconstructs the cute autonomous blob and comes to one definite conclusion: only Astra's conceptual intellect could've created it. Who else would think to make such an impossible creature of water and metal?

The silver globes turn a violent shade of red and a blinding vermilion light washes over her. The figure gives a single beep, its spheres return to a lustrous grey, and it shuffles off.

Automatically Wise follows it. The small bits of greenery yield to sand and the tiny rocks grow into a towering endless expanse of caves. The creature swerves and Wise follows it into one of many identical caverns.

She steps into the mouth of the cave, the light of the dawning sun trailing on the edges of her vision. As she walks deeper the glow rapidly fades away, immersing her in a blackness swiftly withered by the creature's soft blue illumination. The lit-up passageway twists and turns, swallowing them both down a flight of stairs.

Attentively she treads down into the depths. Her chest tightens; her breaths become laboured; her mouth goes dry; her ears swell and block out the sound of her straining inhales and exhales.

The rocky ground gradually consumes the stairs until they merge. Wise stumbles forward to where the glow of cyan shines on a metal door.

The creature's globes emanate a scarlet light that dies when the entryway opens with a flourish.

Wise sees the way out of the confining area and bounds into a bright, vast space of computers and desks, where incomplete thoughts are papered high and low on the cavern's walls. She walks towards the closest wall, and her fingers trace over incomprehensible words whose familiar jumble brings painful tears to her eyes. The writing blurs.

'HEY, HI, WISE.' A vibrant voice rings in her ears.

Wise screeches and spins around. Her back slams into the wall. Then her vision returns to normal as she is met by a familiar presence: a rapturous vivacity stuffed into a plain white lab coat.

'Motion detectors summoned me here,' Astra enthuses. 'Ohhhhhhh, what do you think of Moxie, my little water blob? I made him after the rest of the team departed.'

With a simple flourish of her hand she gestures to Moxie, but Wise's attention is solely on Astra. Long tendrils of blue hair gathered into a messy ponytail, a smile wide enough to crack her face in half, and enough energy to power a city. She hasn't changed a bit, yet so much has changed.

'It's dextrous, functional, and cute. I could tell instantly that it is one of your creations,' Wise curtly replies, as she recites her earlier thoughts and is reminded why she came here.

She reaches into her pocket and shows off the transparent apple core; Astra's face transforms from joyful to stunned to exuberant.

'Although I enjoy our talks about inventions, we've got the matter of saving humanity on our hands—or in this case, literally in them,' Wise says nonchalantly, as she flips the core around in her hand.

'Yes, yes, yes, everything is falling into position.' Astra hops on the spot, her lab coat fluttering around her. 'Science exists for this place and while it can wait, it shouldn't linger. Moxie, lead the way,' she says in a familiar dramatic tone that tugs at Wise's heart. Moxie gives a few beeps and its orbs glow a faint red; the ground in the centre of the room splits open and an elevator emerges. Wise takes one last look at the lab as she crosses the threshold. Then the elevator dings and the view is no more.

The metal box descends slowly and in its grasp the gleaming walls compress her; she leans on the cold, glossy surface and her fists clench as she struggles to breathe.

'Don't worry, we'll be down in a jiffy,' Astra says, giving Wise a cheerful smile. The elevator's metal claws release Wise from their grasp and she can breathe once again.

'I'm so glad I can finally show you this place. You'll be amazed at the equipment we have. This is one of the most sophisticated labs in the modern world and is staffed by the most brilliant minds—or in this case, mind,' Astra says, but her cheery smile seems to be straining. Wise's gaze drifts to Moxie and back to Astra. A lump forms in her throat; her ears feel like they've become stuffed with cotton.

'It must have been a hard adjustment for you when everyone left,' Wise comments, and Astra shakes her head.

'You would think so, but the upper floors remind me so much of that base we built together in primary school that, even empty, it felt like you were about to burst in at any moment,' Astra says ruefully. The lump in Wise's throat disappears, and she can feel her cheeks flush as she mulls over Astra's observation, and lets out a chuckle; a smile plays on her lips.

'Now that you mention it, besides the size and the walls, it did look eerily similar to the old base.' Wise's smile slowly curdles as her happy memories lead her down a dark path. Silence hangs in the air as her ears pop.

'Yeah, the collapse was bad,' Astra remarks, picking up on the line of thought Wise had gone down, 'but, if that didn't happen, we never would have fallen for the beauty that is science.' Her chipper tone lifts the gloom.

'Still seeing the bright side, huh,' Wise says mirthfully.

'Someone has to.' The elevator clunks, dings, and the doors open with a whoosh.

Wise steps out onto the white tiles of the lower lab, and is welcomed by the intimate, comforting scent of sanitiser. The air is filled with the homely sounds of snoring machines, and a few steps in front of her resides a hodgepodge of a computer with levers and knobs that coalesce into its plastic shell. The machine is connected to three conjoined gargantuan metal canisters, two closed and one wide open, all surrounding Astra.

'Place the core into the third canister and...' Astra makes a drum roll sound to Wise's actions, '...Pull! The! Lever!' Wise steps forward and drops the apple core into the open container, which gobbles it up. She heads for the computer and begins the extraction process for the solution. Machines around them whirr, hum, and beep, as they come out of slumber. Her hands move furiously on the keyboard, the clicking sounds echoing off the metal skulls of the computer's brain, which line the walls. She presses 'Enter' and the word 'Denied' flashes across the screen in blaring, confusing red.

'I thought you said it was ready?' Wise hits the keys and re-enters the code into the computer.

'No, I didn't.' Astra's eyes flicker side to side. 'I might have accidentally implied it, but I never said it was ready.'

Wise lets out a soft groan and glances to Astra, who doesn't even have the audacity to look ashamed at her lack of preparation.

'What part of the process needs to be finalised? It better be on the computer; chemicals and I don't mix.' A thoughtful expression flutters over Astra's face.

'Actually, yeah, it's...' Astra clicks her fingers in realisation. 'For the formula to be complete we need an extraction of the tumour in my brain.' Because of Astra's exuberant inflection, it takes a moment for Wise to realise the significance of Astra's words.

'That'll kill you.' Wise's hands clatter dead on the keyboard.

'Err, either I die now or I die later from the tumour,' sighs Astra. 'This is how it goes. You're alive; you get infected by Con-Gio 20 that shuts down your body and eats away at you. Create a vaccine that fails. Remove your brain with the help of the creature you made, then your brain is put in a jar. You live as a hologram for a while. Find a tumour in your brain; find out the cure for the failed vaccine is in the tumour. Extract it; you die again and save the world. Circle of life,' Astra says cheerfully. 'Now pull this switch, press that knob, and humanity is saved—hooray.'

'No.' Wise steps away from the computer, distress leaking into her tone, her attention now solely on Astra.

'Shouldn't that be a yes?' Astra's joking smile turning apprehensive the longer Wise goes without answering.

'Why would you ask me to do this? Why ask me to come here? You had to know what I would say!'

Astra's eyes hold her gently in a way she had once before. Then Wise realises.

'You did...' Wise trails off, '...why?'

Astra's bright attitude falls away into candour, and she materialises in front of Wise.

'Because you're my friend.'

That single sentence explains everything, feeding a soothing pill to the raging acid inside of Wise. But her indignation burns through the medicine, and caustic bubbles rise in her gut.

'You don't get to do this. I won't let you sacrifice yourself just so this world can return to normal for everyone else and spiral into insanity for me!'

Astra gives a shake of her head, and her eyes look so hopeful and bursting with love that Wise chokes on words she has yet to say.

'This world can't return to normal, because the normal that we had was precisely the problem,' Astra says, gently. 'People are dying in the streets. Thousands of refugees have been sent to camps to die. Families left to starve in their homes—no security, and no thought for their wellbeing. That's not the normal I want, but I can only bring us so far as I am; I'm not a person anymore, just a memory of one. I can't grow, I can't learn, I can't touch, but you have these gifts. So you have to go the rest of the way for me and everyone else. You're Wise after all; there's no one else like you, and there's no one else who can do this.'

Wise closes her eyes; hot tears fall down her cheeks, and she runs her fingers through her short greasy black hair.

'Your optimism is tenacious.' She opens her wet eyes, seeing now how Astra's form flickers. She lets her hands fall to her front, clasping one another. 'I hope I can carry it in the same way as you.'

Astra's holographic hands phase through hers, and Wise swears, even with all the evidence to the contrary, she can feel the warmth of them. How she missed her warmth.

'Are you ready?' Astra moves to her side. Wise lets out a sigh and steps forward.

'No. But while science can wait, people cannot.' Wise gives a tiny smile that makes it halfway to her eyes. Then she places her hand on the lever, wrenches it down and pushes the knob simultaneously.

'I really wish I could see the new world with you.'

'Same,' Wise answers, all the while keeping her sights on Astra's flickering form. Specks of golden light ebb off her until all that remains in the room is Wise, Moxie, and the machines. With a few clicks on the computer, Wise takes humanity's future in her hands and by Moxie's glow leaves the underground lab, walking towards the rising sun.

Emilia Rose

Up in the hills where no one goes, lives a girl named Emilia Rose. Before the snow and after the sow, she heads down the mountain to the brow.

When the townspeople spot her a murmur grows, which rises to a cry in a chant that goes: 'What shall remain of you, Emilia Rose? You're perfect down to your toes. You shouldn't be alone to wither and stow; please stay, Emilia Rose.' She ignores the town's crows; up the Mountain she goes, to teacakes and her two cats, named Lisa and Mose.

Time strays and from the mountain she goes. The townspeople always propose: 'What shall remain of you, Emilia Rose? You're perfect down to your toes. You shouldn't be alone to wither and stow; please stay, Emilia Rose.'

Their repetitive crows grow after each sow, and she can no longer ignore her foes. So she strays from the mountain path, leaving behind cake and cats for the strath.

In the square grounds she expounds her life to the town, and she drowns in the show of gowns and frowns; for their crowns are firmly stuck in the ground, and it seems her words are just sounds.

Tired she flees back to Mount Woe, to her teacakes and her two cats, named Lisa and Mose.

When the townspeople see her they once more propose, 'What shall remain of you, Emilia Rose? You're perfect down to your toes. You shouldn't be alone to wither and stow; please stay, Emilia Rose.' She smiles and does not bother to explain; they don't understand her domain.

For on top of Mount Woe she is not alone. She has herself, her cats, and cake. That she will never forsake.

The Possession of Petronella

A mass of motley screeches forces Lyne and Raina out of the room. Raina embraces the placid white walls of the hallway, while Lyne tumbles to the ground. With a loud bang the mayhem inside the room gulps and swallows the door shut, leaving a vacuum of fright and echoes of screams.

'That didn't go as well as I thought it would,' Raina says as she gazes pensively at the door.

'I told you,' Lyne says from her prone position.

'No matter.' Raina turns to her friend. 'We just need to re-group, re-plan, and re-strategise. To the living room, for a partial roommate meeting.' Raina's bloody fingers leave red tendrils up the wall as she shakily gets to her feet.

Seeing Lyne's vacant stare, Raina hauls her up by the back of her turquoise pleather jacket, going from the hallway to the living room with a few drags and a thump.

'It's apparent that we're not equipped to handle this situation. We need help from a higher power to save her,' Raina declares. Her mind whirs; her pink rhinestone-encrusted phone meets her hand, and she begins her journey on the internet. She puts in a variety of phrases in the search engine; the words blur, but she knows it's right even if her eyes can't match her frenzied thoughts. The results show repeats of her questions, ads, and porn. She continues to type away. Intruding at the corner of her eye, the light of the sun drifts down on the ivory wall, and the clock that hangs above the fireplace moves its hands. But they betray her reality: time is stuck for her. She runs her fingers through her short limp pink hair and bites her lip, releasing it in a sigh.

'Do you know anyone we can call?' Raina asks, crouching down to Lyne's level and putting her phone away in her yellow jacket pocket.

Lyne swats her hand at Raina, as one would shoo away a fly. 'Let's just leave her. This is her problem, not ours,' Lyne says as she shuts her eyes.

'Were not going to abandon our friend.' Raina shakes Lyne, till with great reluctance she opens her eyes.

'At this point she's nobody's friend. We would need an exorcist to get her back into that state,' Lyne mumbles, and rolls onto her side as Raina stands to digest the information.

'Requesting an exorcist—is that a smart idea? Though with those fancy robes they wear they've got to know something. At the very least, more than we do.' Raina steps over Lyne as she treads up and down the blue carpet contemplating Lyne's joke. After all, solutions come in many forms.

'But ask yourself: when was an exorcist of actual help?' says Lyne. 'They half-arse their jobs and always leave loose ends. What we should get is a demon; they always come through on their part.' Raina can tell it isn't really a suggestion, but the notion tickles her brain and digs deep into her cortex.

'That's a brilliant idea!' Raina replies.

'That was a joke.' Lyne rubs her temples. 'Getting a demon to tame another demon is a terrible idea.'

'Fire and fire equals what?' asks Raina rhetorically. Her finger wags in the air and a grin stretches from ear to ear.

'A shit-ton of fire,' drawls Lyne.

'No! When fire meets another fire, it cancels itself out. It's like when a minus meets another minus; it transforms to become a plus. It's basic maths,' Raina proudly explains.

Lyne stares at her and takes a deep breath.

'First off, you failed VCE maths,' she snarks. 'Second, one is a number; the other is an uncontrollable force of nature that we can barely contain, and could easily get out of hand and burn us till we're nothing more than ash.'

'Don't worry—I'm flame-retardant,' jokes Raina.

'Wait, what? That doesn't make any sense.'

Raina laughs and ploughs out of her march into a series of flamboyant leaps across the floor and down the stairs.

'Come on, Lyne, we've got work to do!' Raina shouts at her.

'It was a joke! Didn't you hear me when I said—what I am saying, you didn't—Ahhh...' Lyne is in a huff now. 'I'm going to sleep; leave me out of this illegal demon summoning,' she says, and rolls over onto her face.

Raina bounds back up the stairs, grabs Lyne by the foot and starts to drag her tawny-brown figure across the floor.

'Nope, not going to happen. I need someone to hold the book while I catch my rhymes, and your tiny hands are perfect for the job,' Raina says fiercely. Lyne groans and grumbles as she's pulled across the carpet at a snail's pace.

'Fine, fine, I will do the thing—just stop dragging me. I don't want to get carpet burn again.'

Raina drops Lyne's foot with a thunk, and gradually Lyne rolls up and joins Raina on her short descent into the storage space. Raina bolts around the old exercise equipment, tools, tables of found things, and mounds of ancient electronics, heading to the other side of the room, where stacked ancient tomes cover the wall.

'Where did I last see it? Come on, old occult-phase memories, don't fail me now,' Raina mumbles to herself. Her fingers prance along the colourful broken spines. Her eyes gorge on each title as she moves down and across in her search. She lets out a gasp as she pulls out the faded, familiar brown opus. The title jumps out at her in golden script: *Manu Artis Eocatis*. She cracks the spine and flicks through its worn pages to land on a brightly inked five-point celestial sigil.

'And you said I should donate my aunt's old books when I inherited her house,' Raina says smugly, pulling out a piece of chalk from a pile of small rocks and other found things.

'Yes, I very much did, and I still think they should go to the op-shop.'

Raina ignores Lyne's words and plants herself on the ground between the window and the stack of VCRs. Ferociously, she cuts into the black tiles with her white blade of chalk. She can feel Lyne's grey eyes boring into her, and her shoulders tense up.

'What is the price of this help?' Lyne asks with a frustrated sigh.

'When I first read it, the wording was painfully confusing, and now it still brings that same confusion,' Raina says with confidence, hoping against all odds that Lyne won't hear her words and just the tone.

'You have no clue what the price is, then?' Lyne lets out a grump of a hum and Raina stops in her construction and looks up from her sigil.

'Before you go off on a tangent, I know it's dangerous to summon a demon without knowing the price, but I need to help her; she's done so much for me and for you. Saving you from internet trolls and rescuing me from my Mum. She always takes action when we're in trouble; now it's my turn.'

'This is repayment, then?' Lyne asks, and Raina shakes her head violently.

'There is no debt in friendship. She's our friend and you help friends; it's why I made all those cakes last night.' Raina traces the words on the page.

'But to go to this extreme seems excessive, and extremely dangerous.'

Raina whips her head up. She gives Lyne a glare that makes the world fuzzy, and a tiny migraine sprouts at the back of her head, begging to be released. Lyne holds up her hands in a familiar gesture, and Raina waits for her friend to explain herself.

'I'm just saying you don't have to do this,' Lyne says at last. Raina's features relax and her headache dissipates.

'I know,' Raina taps the pages of the book, 'but I want to. I hate seeing my friends in pain.' Raina gives Lyne a playful smile. Lyne closes her eyes and massages her temples, her face in deep concentration. She opens her eyes to meet Raina's gaze. 'The gamble you're making is dangerous.'

'Correction: it's a risk, not a gamble.' Raina places the chalk down and checks her pockets.

'I don't think you know what risk means.'

'Pass me your blade, will you?' Raina asks, ignoring her once again.

Lyne removes her switchblade from her turquoise jacket pocket and throws it at her. It sails straight through Raina's hand, hits her on her milky forehead, and bounces off onto the ground. Blood races down her face and taints the white chalk streaks with red splotches. Lyne's eyes widen, her hand frozen in a throwing motion.

'That's one way to skin a cat,' Raina jokes. She makes sure to give Lyne a big smile, ignoring the pain that now stings her forehead. Now isn't the time for Lyne to feel bad for her, those emotions are reserved for Della. The best thing is to cut them off before they can register in her friend. Lyne reacts to the joke by rolling her eyes in her typical way, and Raina gets off the ground, circles over to Lyne and places the book in her hands.

'Now let's begin.' Raina spins her hands around one another at a steady pace.

'Oh flesh of old and teeth of sharp steel,

Come into our world to forge with us a deal.

We bring sense; we bring soul; and we bring solicitude.

We pull and twist and break and forge this bond in certitude.

Oh hands that are scarred; oh hands that create; oh hands that unwind.

We bring the thread; we bring the steel; we bring the ever-present mind.

The time is right; the time is now, as I've
created this seal.

Come into this world to make a deal.'

Invisible wires burrow in her hands; the
sensation goes from annoying to excruciating. She
breaks the spin, throwing her hands over the
chalked star. The sigil feasts on the concrete and
slashes agape as if torn by dragon claws. Cascades
of ultramarine light maul out of the crevice, and
devour away the cream colouring of the chamber.
A distinct odour of withering flesh fills Raina's
nostrils, and a figure made of fine edges emerges
from the cyan.

'*Why do you bleed? What do you need?
What misdeed do you plead*?'

'Pleasure to meet you, Demon of Threads. I
need your hands to help me—well, not me

exactly, but...' A thump and a scream explode from the ceiling, shattering the conversation.

'*A familiar woe that I know. Just point the way so I can slay.*' The Thread Demon curls a cerulean finger around her chin, and Raina notices the long, jagged scars that litter her hands before they ease back to her sides. A thump of happiness spreads through her chest. This demon is perfect.

'Awesome, what's the price for your help? I couldn't understand what it was when I read it.'

'*A bone from your head truly would suffice. A molar from the back shall be nice.*' That is not what she was expecting, but she has her superb ability to bargain and she can definitely tempt a demon.

'Perhaps I could interest you in another form of payment? Chocolate ice-cream cake, carrot cake, red velvet cake, strawberry cake...'

'*I do not mind the damage. An imperfect bone shows travel, happiness for those who live lavish,*' the Thread Demon says, cutting off Raina's sentence with her scissors made of rhyme. Lyne releases a grating cough. On sheer instinct Raina turns to Lyne, who closes the book and with a single raised eyebrow tells her: I told you so.

'The risk I took was calculated, but man, am I bad at maths,' Raina says sheepishly, giving a nonchalant shrug. Lyne throws the book at her, but it soars past her and lands with a thud on the ground. Lyne could never hurt her on purpose.

'Where are the pliers I need to rip this molar out of my head?' Raina skips around the room and rummages in various piles, and finds the tool. She eyes the pliers apprehensively, then glances away, but she relents, picking up the metal menace in a sweaty hand.

'*Before we begin and before you end, I need to see the one who needs my hand, for returns aren't appreciated by me; it would be a pain for both sides, I decree. Show me the demon we need to defeat so I can go back into the deep.*'

'Will do.' They march up the stairs, back to the threshold that contains the host of the chaos. Raina braces herself and opens the door.

The ground is quilted with millions of discarded, colourful threads. A flood of crumpled tracing paper extrudes from the epicentre of mayhem that is Della, wearing a musty black dress and huddled in the far corner of the room by the small broken domestic sewing machine. Frantically she casts line after line of thread, and with desperate, tedious speed, the fabric glides up and away from her. It is a garment, adorned with millions of tiny sequins, that shimmers across the swallowed benches and entraps Della in a world of cotton and fibre.

'Della,' Raina says, but her words drown in the torrent of thread meeting fabric.

'PETRONELLA!' Raina screams out her full name. That always gets her attention.

Della falls backwards. Fabric lands, haloing her head, and makes a disgruntled, greasy, furious saint out of her.

'Look who I brought you! A sewer, a colour theorist, and look she has crafting hands. Just look how scarred they are.' Raina thrusts the Thread Demon's hands into Della's line of sight. 'She can help you.' The Thread Demon steps past the threshold and stands proudly in front of Della's crumpled form.

'*I have seen many like you who have fallen into threaded time. I can help for a dime, so this moment will become nothing more than forgotten time.*'

Della rolls into a kneeling position in front of the Thread Demon.

'I'll pay anything for your help!' Della says desperately. 'What do you want? I'll give it to you—my soul, my mind, my body. It's yours.'

'*Not you. My dear summoner pays my dues.*' The Thread Demon turns to Raina. '*As she*

confirmed what I need to know, my payment, then
services are ready to go.'

'Oh, right.' Raina pulls out the pliers, opens her mouth wide, and the metal teeth surround her back molar. She closes her eyes and pulls, but the pain stops her at each wrench. She can see Della's wide-eyed joy narrow and slowly morph into a piercing glare at each failed attempt to extract the payment. Raina wants to say she's trying, but there are pliers in her mouth.

'Give me that. Thread Demon, hold her still.' Della grabs the handles. The demon wraps her claws from Raina's shoulders to her hands in a smothering grip, and Della pulls.

Raina's fibres shred in torment as steel gorges on bone ruthlessly. Flesh unpicks from nerve at an excruciatingly sluggish pace that brings rise to sharp pinpricks that needle up her throat and tear out of her in screeches, shrieks, and screams.

'THAT IS ENOUGH,' Lyne shouts. Her words reverberate around the room and the pain is no more. Raina slowly opens her eyes to the sight of Lyne holding the pliers above her head, and Della's expression of disbelief crumples into rage.

'I NEED TO FINISH THIS,' Della growls, reaching out for the pliers.

'Why, huh?' Lyne asks as she fights her off with a glare. 'Just give me one good reason you need to finish this course and I'll let you have the pliers back and mutilate our friend. Our good friend whom I don't like seeing in pain. Our friend who does crazy, stupid stuff—like making cakes at 2am to give you a sugar boost, and illegally summoning demons—that could land her in jail if the wrong people found out. All to help you when you're in over your head drowning in fabric, and in return you drag her down into the depths with you. So just utter that one reason. Come on, say it.'

Della opens her mouth, but not a word tumbles out. Raina looks hesitantly between the two. Words appear in her mind but they refuse to emerge from her mouth. She must let her friends have this conversation, even though she despises that it's happening in front of her. She'll wait for their spat to be done with, and then speak her piece.

'You know why you can't answer! Because fashion isn't worth any of this pain and suffering, I know it and now I'm telling you!' Lyne's grip relaxes and she lets the pliers fall to the ground. 'Just stop being so stubborn and tell me what you want to do.'

Della's scarlet skin strangles against solemn white as her anger cools.

'I want to quit,' Della whispers.

'Then quit,' Lyne says in exasperation.

'I CAN'T, I CAN'T, I CAN'T!' Della screams, rage rolling off her in violent waves. 'IF I GIVE UP NOW, THE TIME I SPENT, THE MONEY I

WHITTLED AWAY, THIS PAIN I'M FEELING, IT WILL ALL BE FOR NOTHING!' Tears pour down Della's cheeks and Raina plants her hands firmly on Della's soft, red, watery face.

'Quoting a wise candy man: "*Giving up now won't make these emotions...* ummmm... what's the word?... *pointless... but I think it will free you from them,*" Raina slurs, blood dribbling down her lips.

'And we waste money all the time. Remember when Raina bought a cotton candy machine?' Lyne says, clearly trying to comfort Della using her straightforward logic, though Raina can't help her outrage at being used as an example.

'Hey, I stand by that machine and the days I spent on gathering a few specks of sugary sweetness,' Raina says, spitting blood all the while.

Lyne whips a piece of calico off the ground and dabs at the blood on Raina's face. Della stares at them and she lets out a chuckle that becomes a sob, that transforms to vicious inhales and exhales, petering out into gasps. To Raina it looks as if she is expelling all of the anguish in her body.

'But I... I... I...' Della says, choking up. Tears trickle down her face as she looks at the pair of them, and Raina knows she's on the edge and all she needs now is a silent push. Raina gives her a warm grin and, giving a little nudge to Lyne, she gives a crooked smile.

'I... quit.' Della's tears dry up, a smile blooms wide on her face and Raina wraps her arms around Della.

'I'm glad to have you back.' Della's arms coil around her.

'I'm sorry,' Della whispers.

'That's okay,' Raina replies, indulging in the closeness she had missed over those long harsh months when her friend was a slave to the needle and thread.

'*Although nothing has changed, travel, time and my mind you've consumed. Payment is needed or else you are doomed,*' the Thread Demon says, disrupting the hug between Della and Raina. The Thread Demon lifts a claw to her mouth and narrows her yellow eyes; it reminds Raina of a predator looking at prey.

Raina's ears swell with pressure, her heart convulses, her mouth runs dry, and her molar throbs once more.

'Would you take a cake as your summoning fee?' Raina fearfully asks. She knew it hadn't worked before, but maybe it would now— time does change people and demons. With a raise of its eyebrow, the demon ponders and the sound of Lyne's palm meeting her forehead echoes across the room. Dread creeps further up Raina's spine each moment the demon remains in what can only be false contemplation.

'*Acceptable, but for your sake they had best be delectable.*' The Thread Demon releases Raina from her grasp. Raina lets out a sigh of relief and Lyne slams her into a hug.

'Never do this again,' Lyne tells her.

'What part? Because…'

'All of it,' Lyne says, interrupting her.

'Can't do that,' Raina tells her flatly. 'You're my friends. I would summon a hundred demons, and pull out all of my teeth for your happiness.'

'I would try to stop you.'

'Yeah, that's apparent.' In a single line, the cavalcade departs from the disarray of the room and into the kitchen, where Raina enjoys the sight of cakes, the company of her friends as they tend to her wounds, and the Thread Demon's rhymes.

Mooro

It all started on a Thursday night when the fires began. News spread and I called my sweet young Anne.

'Don't worry; we've got a plan. Just sit tight and don't come to Shan,' says my sweet young Anne whose words die in my hand. In the night my thoughts clang and demand that I think of those in the strand, my friends, family, and my sweet young Anne. Friday comes, I craft a plan and I head off to Shan.

Driving home, the concrete roads transform to naked earth; my jeep sputters and smokes, the fumes growing in girth. The jeep dies far from the firth, leaving me deserted in the middle of Perth.

I step out and stare at the perverse red ebb, which was once the blue sky, absent of clouds and birds, all gone without a single goodbye.

'My sweet young Anne is far away, safe and alive,' I say to the moon as it arrives—though I find the earth still thrives with heat and smoke as I gather my supplies. Off into the night I search and squawk for allies, but instead I find only those without eyes. Warped flesh and burned bone tell of their demise.

The sun peeks out, rising from its bed, and the surging red spreads up ahead. Growing parched, all I feel is dread, for I can only find the dead. Lost in the brunt of the red I retread, for I know there's nothing but the dead up ahead.

Traveling back the sun bites and takes my might, but soon to my delight I come across a familiar sight and I reunite with the one who brought me to this plight.

I stumble and fall into a heap beside my broken jeep. My eyes grow heavy with sleep. I hear a scream that morphs to a weep; and I swear it's my sweet young Anne, as I fall into sleep.

Floundering, Falling, Flying

As I jump up and down on the roof, the sound of clacking resonates in my ears, the anthem to my tale. Sweat emerges on my forehead; my knees feel weak; my jeans chafe my thighs; my ankles are burning. The sun glares at me: it wishes me harm, wishes me to fail, wishes for my doom. The trampoline appears in and out of sight as I go up and down; it's saying that it will catch me, but I know it's a lie.

'Glasson, jump off already, I'm visibly ageing out here.' Harold's exasperated voice buzzes around my head.

'I'm just psyching myself up!' I yell as I jump into his line of sight.

'You're stalling.' Harold mutters his words in a singsong way.

'I'm not stalling,' I call back in the same tone. Harold lets out a huff and his lips pinch together. I hate when that expression creeps on his face; it makes me want to punch him in his pudgy stomach.

'You've been doing this jumping thing for an hour now. People who are trying to psych themselves up take a few minutes then jump; people who stall cause themselves and others to age.'

I want to reply but I can't; my words are stuck in my throat. My gaze drifts from him, but he moves to match the turn of my eyes.

'Come on—we've all done it and no-one got too badly hurt. Remember, that was Pete's own fault for not wearing the ice-cream bucket during magpie season. *"Green will clash with my outfit and ruin the whole aesthetic look."* You know what else clashes with orange satin? Feathers.'

He stares at me with those soft brown eyes that loop around my being, trying to pull me off; but I remain on the roof, jumping up and down. Harold let's out a sigh, rolls his eyes, slicks back his black curls and clicks his tongue. A grin saunters across his face that makes my stomach twist.

'There's only one way down, because I've taken the ladder. You're going to have to jump eventually—and I've got nowhere to be, so I can watch you do this all day,' he says with a light chuckle. I roll my bottom lip between my teeth and wipe the sweat away from my face as a cool refreshing breeze floats on by. I jump again and again, never leaving the spot I'm in; I feel like a broken clock that won't stop ticking between two places.

Harold gives out a loud, dramatic sigh and tugs on his green top.

'I don't get what you're so afraid of. Just jump off the roof and you're...'

'Falling.'

'...flying; you will be flying. You really need to ditch this fear of yours that once you jump off you will go splat. You're going to be fine,' Harold says sweetly.

I jump higher.

'Well there is a reason for the fear to exist...'

My ankle gives way—I bounce on the blue roof; I watch; I can't stop; I'm a spectator in my own body; I go over the gutter; I'm falling; I'm falling; I'm falling... I'm flying.

Spinning upwards above the ground, I indulge in the strange feeling of weightlessness. On the earth there is a connection; water has a weight; but the air flows across my body as if it were a fine cold sheet on a summer's day.

'See, it's easy,' Harold says as he floats on by in a pose that screams: I am a little shit and you can't do anything to me.

'Well, now I'm upside down—how do I turn? How do I do anything?' I ask, as I scissor-kick in the air sporadically, still staring at the trampoline.

Harold takes out an imaginary cigarette, lights it up and puffs in the fake poison.

'All you've got to do is go with the flow.' He blows out the imaginary smoke.

'Go with the flow, huh, go with the flow,' I mutter to myself as I feel for the breeze. I bring my legs into the current and I slowly start to swim, working out how to move and how to stop; I lose my breath at the power I've gained, at how easy it is to fly. The elation spreads to my face and turns into a grin.

'You're a natural at this. Come on, Mary and the others are probably waiting for us or turned to dust.' He soars up into the sky and I follow behind him, my breath returning to me. We rise past the businessmen and women, the homemakers, the travellers and the birds with whom we share the sky; and I close my eyes, just feeling the air and the sun that caress my cheeks.

'Hey, don't close your eyes!' Harold shouts.

'I was just enjoying myself. Don't worry—I'm not going to become a cautionary tale.'

'That's not why I wanted you to open your eyes. Look.' I turn away from him and see the promised place, Mary's Diner in the Sky. It had only been described to me in the past as a floating bird's nest, and the description is accurate. Doors of unique hue, old indecipherable signs and planks of bent wood forms its circular exterior, and makes the grey landing pad that lines up with the glass entrance stand out against the weathered timber. Landing, my heart beats loud in my chest, my footsteps thud on the concrete, and I breach through the doors; an explosion of rainbow confetti, congratulations, and laughter hits me, making my checks ache in a pleasant way. The cheers peter out into chatter and the tornado of confetti turns to a drizzle; I see how the inside reflects the outside. Though now I can enjoy air conditioning and better company.

'You finally made it, Glasson,' Mary says, cleaning a cup on her white apron as I take a seat at the bar made of sticks and mud.

'Yeah, only took her five years and in the end it was her lack of coordination that got her here,' Harold mentions, as he takes a seat beside me.

'It had nothing to do with my lack of coordination! My feet just went from under me, that's all.'

'So... what Harold said?' Mary chuckles, her green eyes lighting up, and I bite back a frown.

'Can I have my treat now?' I ask, wanting to put an end to the conversation.

'Sure, sweetheart.' She brings out a glass from behind the counter, filled to the brim with chocolate milk and with a dash of whipped cream on top.

'For making it all the way to the nest, here's a drink on the house.'

I lift the milkshake to my lips and the sweet frothy goodness meets my tongue. The muddy lumps fill my vision but quickly drains away till all I'm left with is an empty glass.

Three o'Clock in the Sewing Room

The blue and green fabrics converge under the metal foot and they meet intimately. The needle is thrust into the fibres and Ebony pushes down on the pedal; the sword pierces the fabric in rapid succession. The black thread pulls through, binding the fibres into one piece. A click of the pedal and the filaments are severed. Ebony repeats the monotonous cycle as the colours of the fabric blur together and her wrist burns. She rubs her eyes and rolls her sore shoulders, her body demanding rest; with a flick of her finger, the machine dies under her hands. She stares at the piles of unsewn squares that cry for form, and disregards them to indulge in her lethargy.

'Why isn't this working?' Jemma moans, as she wrinkles the cloth in her smothering hold, hiding the fault from all eyes, even her own. 'I want to take a break, but I can't, because I won't stop thinking about this wretched thing. It's a horrid dilemma.' Despair is smeared across her face. Tears of frustration well in her eyes and threaten to spill over.

Ebony knows the mantra intimately, having reflected it from inside and out over the year. The original 25 students have been slashed and cut to three exhausted, frustrated, greasy-haired, caffeine-addicted zombies, and one clear-skinned, relaxed Melody.

Jemma's tears flow down her pimpled cheeks; her sobs thunder in the cramped sewing room. Ebony tries to think of a comforting word or phrase that could spark a reminder of Jemma's goal, her dream. Something that might hold back the flood of misery and let her continue to create... but what is Jemma's dream? They each said it at the start of the year when they introduced themselves. What had Jemma said? Ebony can't recall the start of the year. It seemed to be nine years ago rather than just nine months.

So, lost for a caring remark, Ebony ignores Jemma's despair and turns instead to the ticking hands of the clock that proudly proclaim 1:00 pm. She wonders if she should go off into the cutting room to escape the clamour and finish her project in the adjoining space. But the move, the set-up, and the threading problems that are sure to occur would only hamper her, not help.

'Why the un-needed worry, Jemma?' Melody asks from her reclining position on the table by the door, typing mindlessly on her phone. 'It's just TAFE, not uni; we're not getting graded or anything. Just hand in something and if you can't, well, there's always next year.' Jemma's cries soar and plaster the room in her despair;

55

Melody's attempt at comfort has fallen flat in what Ebony can only assume is ignorance.

'You do know that this course is being discontinued at the end of the year? If we fail, we have to transfer to a new school,' Devein says, unpicking his sleeve, which he had sewn to his misshapen red top, yet again.

The clatter of fingernails on glass stops. 'What?'

'Haven't you read the emails the school sent out?' Devein asks in disbelief.

'Nope,' Melody says, popping the p'. 'Due to a disagreement with the school I am not receiving anything related to this course.'

Ebony briefly entertains the notion of asking her the story behind that, but quickly abandons that thought. Knowing Melody, it was a silly stupid reason that escalated beyond all bounds of common sense.

'Well, if you had received them,' Devein says, 'you would know that at the end of the year the Advanced Diploma of Fashion and Technology is being discontinued. If we don't finish our work today and hand it in to "I-do-not-give-extension" Mrs Klee at six, we will not graduate and will have to re-enrol elsewhere, to a place that will probably declare our knowledge from here insufficient for their institution and we'll have to go through this whole nightmare all over again.'

Melody doesn't reply, remaining eerily quiet. Gradually her loose form rises off the table. Her eyes shift from side to side, her left leg jitters, she bites her manicured nails and tugs at her green locks.

'Miss Dontoni, hmmm, work, hmmm, seen,' Melody murmurs… and in a flutter of Ebony's eyelid, she races out of the open door and out of sight down the hallway.

'What does she think she's doing?' Devein says, adjusting his glasses. 'It's too late to start. The illustrations, C.A.D., Photoshop, spec sheets, costings, pattern-making, sewing... I give up on this sentence—I've got too much work to do.'

'Maybe she'll transfer, but I did hear her say something about Miss Dontoni. She might try to appeal to her,' Jemma thoughtfully adds, taking her handkerchief out of her ratty jeans, drying her tears on the worn blue fabric.

'Well, they've known each other for 12 years, so Melody definitely could persuade her for an extension, though I doubt Miss Dontoni would be able to move Mrs Klee. Course coordinator versus mountain—you know who I'm putting my money on,' Devein retorts; and as the conversation dies, the room returns to silence.

Ebony faces her fabric once again. She hears its silent demands to bring it into being. Giving in, she flicks the switch; the industrial sewing machine hums to life and the ritual begins again. Time only passes in the piles of completed squares and the burning in her wrist that slowly becomes unbearable. With a jab she turns the machine off, and takes a moment of reprieve.

Standing up, Ebony wanders out of the row of industrial sewing machines. She treads the edges of the room in a familiar circuit; passing the table, she tries to snub the clock that's about to appear out of the corner of her eye. Three, it says on its face; the day is almost over, and her project incomplete, yet she can't help but continue her walk.

She drags her feet past the irons, and the forbidden scent of melted cheese and toasted bread emanates from the adjoining solitude space of the cutting room. A violation of the sewing room rules: no food or drink in the area under pain of a pin being eaten. That explained where Melody had run off to. Though why go out, circle around and go through the other door? The aroma disrupts her thoughts and calls her stomach to a ravenous growl, and all she can think of is cheese and bread. Perhaps Melody would share some of the delicious grilled goodness with her, if she puts her words the right way. Ebony backtracks a few steps and grasps the chipped white knob.

Opening the door, she's hit by a furious barrage of heat. Curtains ablaze; the tables alight; the domestic machines melting; the rulers distorting and warping; and the sandwich on the table turning from a toastie to a clump of ash. Ebony retreats and closes the door, though she knows it will only be one hot minute before the fire knocks—and whether or not she answers it will be let in.

'There is a fire,' Ebony says, her stomach doing a somersault. Jemma and Devein remain seated, enraptured by their tasks, unperturbed by her. Ebony starts to sweat. Her breath shortens. Dread boils in her gut and expels in a scream of, 'FIRE!' scalding Jemma and Devein away from their projects.

'Fire?' Devein parrots back at her.

'Yes,' Ebony replies, breathless.

'When you say fi—' Jemma gets cut off by the trickles of smoke that rise from under the door, '...oh, fire, that *is* fire.'

They scramble back to their respective workstations. Ebony scoops her project into her arms. Her classmates follow suit; abandoning hard-worn logic for fashion commonsense, they only flee once their projects are secure.

Together they race down the concrete steps, out through the doors, and they arrive at the car park where the entire school looks on in rapture at the blaze. Ebony stares at the fire that engulfs the entire fashion floor and threatens to spread out and down. The sounds of fire trucks are an anthem to the tempest that currently roars around Ebony.

'Thank goodness you guys made it out all right,' says Miss Dontoni with a checklist in hand. Miss Dontoni counts them off visually, a frown emerges on her face.

'Where's Melody?' Miss Dontoni asks. Ebony shrugs; she knew from the sandwich Melody was in the sewing room, but now her location is a mystery.

'I'm here,' Melody proudly proclaims as she saunters into view, effectively putting an end to the minute-long mystery that she had unintentionally created.

'Well, girls and Devein, as the fire has basically spread to the entire sewing room, it looks like final presentations are cancelled, but you each get a CO as I know you put in the work.'

Ebony hides away her unfinished project and the slight shuffles of her classmates tell her she's not alone in her actions.

'And don't worry about Mrs Klee. I'll handle her if she puts up a fuss about you guys passing; we've got rules for when this happens.' A thoughtful look crosses her face. 'Well, not exactly this, but similar, well, not... basically, the rules can bend around this situation. If you need anything I will be with the fire marshal and hopefully later this evening as well,' Miss Dontoni says, leaving them to their own devices.

'Well at least one good thing came out of this disaster,' Devein remarks.

'How did this even happen?' Jemma asks. The fire trucks sprays water into the inferno that spews black smoke, tainting the air.

'Don't care,' Devein replies.

'Maybe it was... arson,' Jemma suggests jokingly.

Ebony casts her sight away from the scalding flames, landing on Melody, who sweats under her unintentional gaze. 'It is clearly an accident. I mean, what person burns down a sewing room?' Melody jokes in a forced tone, and Jemma lifts her eyebrow.

'How did you know it started in the sewing room?' she asks in a quizzical tone. 'You weren't even there.'

Melody's face goes completely pale. 'Well, I, um… I, ummm,' she stutters, seemingly lost for words.

'You burnt down the sewing room,' Jemma accuses in a flat tone. Jemma, Ebony and Devein surround Melody, boxing her in.

'Noooooooo.' Melody puts up her hands, as if trying to physically stop the train of thought that chugs through her classmates' heads and her own. But you can't stop a train with only a hand.

'Your sandwich was there. No one else eats in the sewing room.' Ebony is adding fuel to the imaginary engines. She wants a verbal confession to sate her newly rekindled curiosity, the literal blaze reigniting the metaphorical fire of life inside her.

Melody shuffles from one foot to another, umming and erring.

'I may or may not have accidentally put the broken radio on, and might have left a piece of calico around the frayed wires—but *if* I did do this, it was to pass this course. And, as an added bonus, so did you guys,' Melody cheerfully confesses.

The crackling of wood and glass are the only sounds to fill the silence. Ebony should be enraged; annoyance should follow next. But the bubbling of warm emotion that begins at her toes spreads up, overtaking her, and out comes,

'Thank you.'

Ebony's gratitude breaks the rising tension and she can see her fiery elation spread to Devein and Jemma. Joy practically radiates off their skin and they pat Melody on the shoulder in silent thanks.

'Since this is our last day, do you guys want to celebrate with some karaoke?' Melody says. 'I've always wanted to try it, but it's just too sad to do it on my own.'

'Since my plans for the afternoon have blown up, I'll join,' Jemma says.

'Me too,' Devein pipes in.

'Sure,' replies Ebony, and in single file they jaunt down the street. While Ebony walks, a little thought worms its way into her head. She hopefully knows the answer, but it's one she must ask for the sake of her own curiosity.

'So, we weren't in any danger?' Ebony asks.

'No. You were,' Melody replies, seemingly high from the elation that had oozed off Jemma and Devein mere seconds ago. 'It is pure luck that you survived.'

Ebony halts. Calling over the police and reporting Melody's destructive actions would be so simple, but what would become of her grades if this got out? A repeat of the year, most likely, all because Melody's brazen attitude incensed her. Weighing the year's torment against Melody's arson, the answer to the situation becomes clear to Ebony, and she continues to jaunt behind her partners in crime.

Miss Gogaerous

Miss Gogaerous stretches her two front legs. The listless flap of a kookaburra's wings stirs her stomach in anticipation and she looks up at the sky that validates her expectations. The barely visible blinking eye of the moon bathes in the glow of the fading sun, which shoots purple rays across the wane of red that blankets the sky in its warmth.

It's the perfect moment, and the only moment in the twilight to swim into the hidden world that resides below. Just imagining it brings a smile to her face. The magical realm that gleams with hidden treasures that can only be encountered if you don't look for them but stumble upon them. The world around her knows not the secrets of the realm below. Those are hers alone.

Miss Gogaerous lets her happy musings about the watery world fill her thoughts and indulges in them, for they are the only suitable sustenance for her arduous journey ahead. She narrows her eyes at the twisted tower in front of her and takes a deep breath.

She clumsily frogs her way onto the first stone of her tower; her 18 toes and tail burn as she leaps onto the scalding rock, but with each jump, the pain steadily recedes as the temperature changes from burning to delightfully warm. The fragrant scent of lilies turns to the sweet aroma of faraway lands, carried by the wind. The trees rustle in a harmonious joyful cheer and the reeds below sway in an exuberant clap as she makes the jump to the peak of her tower.

Balancing on the edge, she peers down at the still water of her gigantic pond. She hears the flies buzz that her pond is nothing more than a puddle; but their truth doesn't matter, only hers. A grin spreads across her face and stings her cheeks as she takes her position.

Miss Gogaerous spins around three times. She closes her eyes, her front legs reach toward the heavens, and her back legs and tail quiver under her weight. She can feel the sun flicker away in the dusk, as though jealous of her.

With a loud splash, water collides with her body. She blinks and spins around to see the cause of this disruption in her less-than-watery world. A ball. Someone has thrown a comically large, luminous green ball into her perfect little pond. The mass engulfs the water from edge to edge and obstructs her way to the other realm.

69

Miss Gogaerous grits her gums and stamps her tail on the rock below. A fever of red fills her body; she thumps the rock three more times till the hurricane of scorching heat in her veins turns to a pleasant hum. She frogs furiously down into the scant amount of water that surrounds the ball. She places her toes on the smooth surface of the intrusion, flaps her tail and painstakingly pushes the globe up to where the water and earth meet. With loud huffs and gruffs, she tries to press it onto the dirt, but gravity pushes back and the ball slams into her over and over again. The sun caresses her back, coaxing her on, but the ball remains in her pond. The hoots of owls and the scuttles of claws on bark emerge, and the comfort of the sun disappears.

Miss Gogaerous turns to see that the moon has risen to give her a mocking wink, laughing from its perch high in the sky. She ignores its glee and returns to her strenuous task.

The sounds of the night vanish. Daylight sparks once again and the moon withdraws its presence, but the sun dies a quick death. The sounds of night re-emerge and the moon makes its glorious appearance full and wide to revel in her defeat, as she lies drowning on top of the cold, immovable mass.

The forest cackles and the ball beneath her shakes and trembles as though afraid. She gives a half-hearted glance around in the moon's incandescence that stretches through the thin forest, and sees nothing. The air picks up around her, whistling sweetly through the leaves and grass as it never has before.

She scrunches her eyes up against the gleam from above, the moon's glow starting to crowd her. She looks down; her mouth goes dry; and her mind goes blank. Her toes penetrate the ball; the outside cracks and breaks under her form and reveals life. The creature looks like a rolled-out fish though elegant in form, even as it struggles against gravity, appearing unsure of where to go.

The shell of the creature disappears beneath the water and erupts into a savage pink light that screams out into the dark. It envelops the night in its mystical radiance of colour and brightness, which would make even the sun jealous. Ferociously, the being tears into the pink abyss and spirals into a strange world of incandescent colours.

Miss Gogaerous strains her eyes in this colourful world, her sight adjusting as the vivacity decreases in hue until it's nothing more than pure black and she is left blind again. The creature soars in the colossal darkness for what could be seconds or millions of years, and Miss Gogaerous stares into the emptiness and searches for life other than her own.

She sees a spark in the moonless void

and the world is rapidly lit up by twinkling stars, milky ways and galaxies, but parts of the dark sky remain bare, creating empty circles in the star-filled heavens. The black pools shimmer and remind her of rain falling into puddles. The oblivion tears, bellowing out colours as creatures of varying shapes and sizes swim beside her in the vast expanse.

Tugs of her legs and tail, one push, the other pull, her legs grow and her tail diminishes. Her body floats up; she and the creatures swim alongside in a haze of mystic colour, into galaxies that sing of untold life and past rivers of planets that decorate the endless sea of black that is the depths of her pond.

The creatures swerve and tumble across the dark in exhilaration. Miss Gogaerous watches, her cheeks burn and her stomach swims at their enchanting movements, but the flapping inside her withers as the creatures become still. Their wings simultaneously expand, shimmer and rise ominously, and with one great thrash of their wings, swirls of colour replace their forms. The only marks of the creatures' presence are the vibrant specks they leave in their wake. Miss Gogaerous follows their trails, but the light diminishes and evaporates in the dark; the stars follow suit.

Miss Gogaerous halts, not knowing where to go without the light to guide her, and floats in the abyss. Her toes grow cold, her eyes become heavy and her nerves become numb. A familiar shine caresses her face and her body awakens under its attention; she hears the light call her and she soars towards it. Breaking through the surface of her pond, she greets the sun.

Resting in the tepid water she stares at the stars hidden under the reds and purples that blanket the sky. A smile spreads over her face as she emerges from the water, and once

again begins her trek to her stone tower for
her twilight flip.

Mr Gilberry

Mr Gilberry of Hubert and Thompson accounting firm is a most typical accountant. If someone were to describe him they would say he fits the mould perfectly. Always seen in a neatly pressed, drab black suit, hair slicked back so that every single strand is controlled, he leaves the office at exactly 5:30 pm. Yes, Mr Gilberry is the most stereotypical of accountants to anyone who looks upon the surface; and if it were not for a new arrival at the firm, no one would really know how peculiar he is.

To young, bright-eyed Jayden Blake, his job is merely a stepping-stone to bigger and greater things, even if he doesn't know what those things are. For now though he has been given the task of entertaining a new client. At first Jayden is excited about charming Mr Peterson, but as the time draws closer and he learns more about him, the excitement is replaced by dread.

From what he has heard, the client has a habit of disregarding social etiquette with those he deems below him, and a burning hatred of just about everything. Jayden's expectations are high for the night; however he realises that if he can make no appeal to Mr Peterson, the client might speak badly of him as an accountant. A few ill-placed words in the wrong ears and bam, he'll be stuck in the same position for the next 20 years.

Can he entertain a client like that and leave unscathed? He can't; he'll be walking into career suicide. He needs to foist this duty upon another. But who would slip into the role and perform it perfectly?

Walking down the hall, a storm rages inside him. He swings his head around wildly, his eyes tracing the golden name plaques decorating the various plain brown doors, wondering who would take this responsibility from him and set him free. Although he could not leave this to any old accountant, he needs someone who can schmooze and charm so that the severe Mr Peterson signs over his assets, no questions asked.

Catching the name Mr Gilberry, he backs up to the door and he can't help the small smile that blooms on his face.

Mr Gilberry is perfect for the job: he is one of the oldest workers at the company and an accountant many admire for his fast-thinking, quick-talking and general no-nonsense demeanour. He can take the client out. No matter what Mr Peterson may say about him, Mr Gilberry will come out unscathed—and, by association, Jayden will as well.

Confidently knocking upon the door, Jayden hears a quiet 'come in'. Opening the door he wields a winning smile and saunters in with confidence.

Mr Gilberry lounges in his oversized brown leather chair, and types away on his ancient computer. His chair should make him look small, but just seems to enlarge him, as though the chair is an extension of his being; he looks up briefly and goes right back to typing. Jayden suppresses a frown, keeping a cheerful smile plastered on his face.

'What do you want, Jayden? I'm very busy and have little time to spend on such a person as you.'

Jayden's hopes are instantly dashed. He thought he had made a good impression on Mr Gilberry the last time they talked, but it seems he is nothing more than a fly buzzing around Mr Gilberry's head. That doesn't bode well for the conversation, but he has already come this far.

Gathering his dwindling confidence, he says,

'Mr Gilberry, I'm wondering if you can entertain Mr Peterson tonight.'

Mr Gilberry looks up from his computer screen. His piercing blue eyes bore into Jayden, who holds his gaze, firmly standing his ground, though every inch of him is shouting to leave and never bother Mr Gilberry again.

'Jayden, may I remind you that I am an internal accountant.'

'I know, but...'

'Maybe you should go back to your community college and take remedial classes on accounting,' Mr Gilberry says, cutting off Jayden's words, 'though I doubt it would help such a man who lacks the mental capacity for understanding such information. Now please leave my office. I have important work to do and I have already wasted more time than I would like on this conversation.' The sounds of typing cut off any future conversation.

Jayden floats out in a daze, feeling as if he is six years old and wearing his dad's suit again.

Looking at his watch he sees the time is 5:30 pm. He can't ask any more accountants to take on Mr Peterson, otherwise they will know Jayden can't handle him. Any hint of deferring his duties at this juncture and he will be permanently stuck in this position till the day he dies. He is officially stuck between a crematorium and an adult bookstore.

Sighing heavily, he walks back to his office to go over his plan for tonight's schmoozing with Mr Peterson, keeping a close eye on the time.

As the clock alerts him that it's 7:55 pm, he exits the office building. Nerves wrack his body as the clock on his wrist ticks over to eight and as expected, a long black limo pulls up to the kerb.

Putting on a false mask of confidence Jayden opens the limo door, slides into the dimly lit interior and shuts the entrance, trapping himself with the small but oh-so-terrifying Mr Peterson. The limo speeds away from the building and Jayden turns to him, laying out the plans for that evening.

'So, Mr Peterson, I think you are really going to enjoy the...'

'I prefer not to know where I am going on such occasions as these,' Mr Peterson interrupts. 'I'd rather be surprised and disappointed later than be disappointed right from the start of the evening. For now, let us sit in silence. I have no need for small talk.'

They sit in awkward, forced silence as Jayden clenches his teeth. The dance between them has only just begun and he's already stepped on Mr Peterson's toes. He needs to slow down and let him take the lead.

As the limo pulls into Lowen Avenue, blue and red lights momentarily blind Jayden. Shielding his eyes from the harsh radiance, he pales at the scene of police cars decorating the front of Lillo Dining Experience.

Jayden turns to Mr Peterson. He expects the client is going to look at him with disgust at his incompetence and shout at him like a disappointed school principal, but instead is pleasantly surprised to see Mr Peterson is distracted by his phone. Jayden lets a silent sigh of relief pass his lips. The small mercy soothes him.

Getting out of the limo quietly, he approaches a police officer standing idle beside the entrance.

'What's happening?' Jayden demands. The cop gives him a scathing look.

'A crime has been committed and the place has been shut down,' the police officer points out in a bored tone, clearly disinterested by the crime.

'No, no, no,' Jayden mutters, wringing his hands together in anguish. 'How did this happen?

This diner is known for its dullness! They have partitions around each table so you don't interact with any of the other patrons; their food is basic and plain. Heck, even all the reviews say that this is the most boring dining experience ever. They even brag about it on their website. I mean, what crime happened in the most boring diner in the world— did the chef's put too much salt in a customer's pasta?'

Before he could continue on his tangent, a gurney passes with a person-stuffed black bag displayed on the top. The police officer raises his eyebrow, giving Jayden a look that clearly speaks the words he cannot bother to say.

Huffing, Jayden walks back to the limo and taps on the driver's side window. The glass slowly opens and the grizzled face of the chauffeur comes into view.

'Can you drive us around till I find another place to take Mr Peterson to dinner?'

'Sure, but I've driven this guy around before and let me tell you, I've never seen him pleased.'

Getting back in the limo, Jayden begins a search on his phone for another boring diner like Lillo, although the results returning to him are all out of the country.

The limo comes to a sudden halt; he goes flying out of his seat, landing face first on the floor. Getting to his knees, he leans against the driver's seat.

'I thought you were a professional,' Jayden moans.

'I am; that's why Pinkie's still standing,' the driver tells him.

'Huh?' escapes from Jayden's mouth. Dragging himself up using the driver's seat he sees what the chauffeur is referring to.

A person smothered in pink is splayed against the limo's hood, wielding a sword. Jayden brings up his phone to call for help, but the figure flees into the night before his fingers can move. He stares, stunned, the strange person playing on his mind.

He swears he knows that face hidden under layers of makeup. The accentuated blue of the eyes, the same colour that bored into him just a few hours ago... that's Mr Gilberry wearing a sparkly pink dress and matching pink stripper heels, and swinging a sword someone would normally find at a Renaissance fair.

Rushing out of the limo Jayden faintly hears Mr Peterson shouting after him, but he doesn't bother to turn around. Getting Mr Peterson's account is a bust; the smart thing to do is save his position at the firm through blackmailing Mr Gilberry about his sword-wielding escapades. He needs clear confirmation in a confrontation video; he just hopes Mr Gilberry's flushed appearance is from intoxication, not from all his rushing around.

Sprinting down the streets Jayden tracks Mr Gilberry's most logical route. Under the harsh glare of yellow streetlights, his muscle inflame, his suit becomes drenched in sweat, his ankles swell, and each inhale and exhale burns till he finally comes to a stop, out of breath, in front of a deserted alley. He can see at the end of it a red light illuminating an equally enchanting red door, which Mr Gilberry must have gone through.

He walks into the boxed-off area. His hand meets the rusty door handle and pulls, then pushes, but it doesn't budge an inch. He knocks on the door; no one answers.

Sighing in defeat, he turns, slumping against the wood, and shock goes through his body as he sees Mr Peterson standing right in front of him, arms crossed over his chest, looking irate.

'Why did you leave in such a rush?' Mr Peterson asks, hostility lacing his tone.

A million yarns race through Jayden's mind, but none seem believable. Mr Peterson taps his fingers on his arm, a sour look decorating his white face as he waits for an answer.

Jayden bites his lip; no lie seems good enough. And the longer he thinks the louder the sound of fabric and fingers become, and he blurts out: 'I thought I saw someone from work.'

Mr Peterson lips thin to a sharp line and his eyes narrow, much like a cat when it's about to strike its prey.

'That's no reason for abandoning me in such a way. It was quite rude of you.' Jayden stands up straight and keeps his would-be retorts close to his chest. As he moves close in the obligatory way to apologise, the door explodes and wood chips shower them both. Something hits Jayden from behind, throwing him onto Mr Peterson, who hits the pavement.

Jayden slowly opens his eyes and lifts his head, squinting through the dust in the air. He gets up off Mr Peterson.

'Mr Peterson, are you alright?' Jayden asks.

'No,' Mr Peterson replies.

Jayden lets out a sigh of relief—obviously he is all right, otherwise he would not be responding to him—but he needs to assess his injuries and see if he needs to be taken to a hospital.

'Ah, let me rephrase that: are you in danger of dying soon or in immense pain?'

'No.'

Helping Mr Peterson off the ground he evaluates his injuries—a few scrapes and soon-to-be bruises. He begins to express his regret to Mr Peterson, but halfway through his second string of apologies he notices that Mr Peterson isn't indulging in his prostration and is instead enraptured by what is behind him. Jayden turns to see what has Mr Peterson so enraptured.

Hundreds of red beady eyes bore into him hungrily. Jayden tries to divert his gaze but the creature's engrossing size demands that he indulge in every crevice of the being. Jayden rakes his eyes over the creature's hard transparent shell, which shows off organs that squirm and convulse, all the way down to its pincers, dripping with blood.

Jayden's mouth goes dry. Every inch of him is telling him to run, but fear holds him tight and he cannot break free from the embrace.

The creature lunges towards him. Jayden closes his eyes as he prepares to feel nothing but blinding agony; warm liquid splashes across his face and he can feel it drenching his suit, but he doesn't feel any pain.

Reluctantly opening his eyes, blood blurring his vision, he makes out a shadowy figure standing on top of the creature and a sword protruding from the beast's head. The figure rips the blade out of the creature and jumps down in front of Jayden. Blinking away the blood to see who has saved them, he is astonished to lay his eyes on Mr Gilberry.

Jayden feels a laugh bubbling up but it gets stuck in his throat. This is perhaps the most peculiar scene he has ever come across in the accounting world, but then again that bar was awfully low in the first place.

'You probably have a lot of questions; do not bother asking, I'm not going to answer them, so you should probably leave right now.' Mr Gilberry walks right past Jayden and Mr Peterson, going through the destroyed door as though he had not just shot through it and killed a creature that had appeared to have swam out of the Mariana Trench.

Jayden cannot leave it like that. If he is never going to move up in the company, he may as well figure out what is going on, so he runs into the darkness after Mr Gilberry.

Turning on the flashlight on his phone to illuminate the way. The floorboards creak underfoot as he walks down a dingy hallway to a bare room and back again. The building twists like an Agatha Christie novel, looping him around. It soon becomes obvious that he isn't going find Mr Gilberry running around like a headless chicken.

Halting, echoing footsteps greet his ears. He listens patiently trying to pinpoint the location. The steps steadily grow louder and louder behind him until they cease. He lets a smile cross his face. He's got him.

He turns around and his excitement curdles into disappointment. It is only Mr Peterson, looking rather... well, Jayden can't describe the expression spreading across the client's face, but he can tell Mr Peterson rarely uses those facial muscles.

'Mr Peterson? What are you doing here?' After the incident with the creature, Jayden expected him to have left, not followed him in—though now he still has a chance at getting his account.

'This night is turning out quite interesting. I could not leave it on such a peculiar note.' Oh that is excitement on his face; no wonder Jayden couldn't read it.

'Mr Peterson, you really should leave. This is dangerous; you could get hurt or worse.' Jayden is trying to appeal to Mr Peterson's sense of self-preservation. His boss would kill him if Mr Peterson dies before he can secure the account.

'And you won't?'

'I'm not head of a million-dollar company, with a million people depending on me,' Jayden reasons.

'You cannot get rid of me; I am far to invested to just leave now.' Jayden can't bother to spout reason and logic at him anymore; it's as if he's talking to a toddler.

'Alright. Just stay close to me, then.' To Jayden's shock Mr Peterson doesn't say a word and follows behind him.

They come across a strange room consisting of long hallways and small rooms, all opening into a theatre. On the stage there's a few old wooden chairs, music stands covered in dust and a large bundled tarpaulin placed in the centre. They scour the room for any sign of Mr Gilberry, but he remains out of sight.

Jayden is silently contemplating what to do next when his phone buzzes to life in his hands, shocking him, and he instinctively declines the call in fright; people who call him are people he never wants to talk to.

The tarp on the stage begins to move, it falls away to reveal another of those creatures. The critter is much like the last one he saw, except much smaller.

Jayden pulls Mr Peterson behind the worn red velvet seats and away from the creature's sight, but too late—he can feel one of its many eyes trained on him.

Looking discreetly up from behind his seat he can see it is ready to attack as it bucks its hindquarters at them. This time Jayden is somewhat prepared; he raises his fists to fight the creature, and vainly hopes that he will make it out of the theatre and not into another.

Then Mr Gilberry swings down from the rafters—and with one swift swish of his sword he kills the creature, much to Jayden's shock and relief. Pulling out the sword with a squelch, he walks to the end of the stage— uncharacteristically fast for a person in heels.

'I was hoping that you were smart enough to leave this place.'

'A person such as me lacks the mental capacity to do what you said.'

Mr Gilberry rolls his eyes at him.

'Maybe you can understand this. Leave now,' Mr Gilberry commands, pointing to a door.

'Explain what these creatures are and we will leave,' Mr Peterson demands as he approaches the stage. Mr Gilberry groans in what Jayden can tell is pure frustration.

'If you must know, I'm part of a secret society of accountants who protect this world from creatures that come from Yonder. Now leave.'

'Yonder? Where is Yonder?' Jayden asks.

Mr Gilberry sighs loudly as he realises that Jayden and Mr Peterson aren't going anywhere without a thorough explanation.

'Have you ever heard of the multi-universe theory?'

'Is that *for every action or inaction we take in our lives it creates a parallel universe*?'

'In its most basic sense, yes,' Mr Gilberry says in exasperation, rolling his eyes in the way that Jayden has seen him do before, when the answer was half right. 'Yonder is a plane of existence that surrounds our realm. It is a coating that protects us from other worldly interference, but within this world are creatures called Nigh that dwell in the sands and can dematerialise and reconstruct at will. They are primitive but incredibly dangerous, and every once in a while a faultline breaks open between the worlds and creatures from Yonder fall through. It is our duty as Knights of Order to protect this world, no matter what the cost,' he explains, as if he is a parent teaching his children how to boil an egg.

'Now leave and be quiet; loud noises attract them. There's only one more of these things here and I can't worry about civilians as I do my job. I have to watch my own back now my partner's gone,' he says looking at his ring wistfully. Jayden catches the embossed letters K.O. decorating the top of the large brass ring.

'You had a partner?' Jayden blurts out, not really in a question. No wonder Mr Gilberry is this way; he's grieving. Jayden feels twinges of sympathy for him.

'No more questions.' His wording is definite and forceful. 'Leave. I have a Nigh to take care of.'

'We will leave, but just one more question. Why accountants?' Jayden asks, slightly confused. He feels like the answer is right on the tip of his tongue but won't fall off.

'Don't you know, Jayden?"

'No, clearly I don't.'

'The core of an accountant is our smarts.' Without a single word more he exits stage right and the world is illuminated. With a click, Jayden's phone meets his pocket.

Left with very little choice, Jayden and Mr Peterson leave the theatre, but finding their way out is harder than it originally seemed. The building is a labyrinth. Every exit leads to a different room and every entry is a dead end.

Filtering down the hallway Jayden hears grunts, a Nigh's screech and the echoes of a sword clanging. Mr Peterson gives Jayden a look, and his own curiosity and the desire for the client's wealth drive him silently down the hall to peek in on the climactic battle.

This Nigh is the biggest of the three. Mr Gilberry is on the ground, drenched in blood of the Nigh and possibly his own—he's wobbling, eyelids flickering and his sword is barely staying erect. The sword's hilt slips from Mr Gilberry's grasp and clatters to the ground. Horror dawns on Mr Gilberry's face as the creature lunges for him.

Jayden rushes onto the stage, and picks up the fallen sword. He jumps, swings and the metal connects. Blood pours from one of the many eyes of the creature; it moans in pain as Jayden continues to hack into it. Finally ending the creature's misery, he plunges the sword into the empty eye socket, and out squirts a torrent of hot red blood over his shoulder. The Nigh gives one last roar and collapses on the stage, twitching as life finally leaves it. Breathing heavily, Jayden hunches over the fallen creature, exhausted from his violent swinging. Mr Gilberry approaches him. He doesn't say a word, but takes the sword out of Jayden's hand and limps away from the scene, disappearing, taking the light with him.

Jayden takes his phone out; he shines the beam around, illuminating the now irate, blood-covered Mr Peterson. Jayden's stomach twists. Following the trail of blood to the exit, Jayden doesn't speak to Mr Peterson. What could he even say to him? An apology wouldn't even be close. This night is a disaster. At the destroyed door they silently part ways. Jayden heads dejectedly home, where he's unable to fall to sleep.

When he gets to his office the next morning he sees Mr Hubert waiting by his office door, large and intimidating—but that might have been the sleep deprivation warping his sense of spatial awareness.

'Mr Peterson told me all about what happened last night, with you and Mr Gilberry.'

Jayden breaks out in a cold sweat. Mr Peterson probably mentioned how he briefly abandoned him, and then covered him in blood.

'What did he say?' He can't help but ask, even though he knows the answer.

'He said the oddest and most out-of-place words that have ever traversed his mouth,' Mr Hubert says rubbing his chin. 'He said that last night was fun.'

'Fun?' Jayden asks, hiding the shock in his voice.

'Mr Peterson is a joyless person and for him to enjoy anything is akin to a fish killing a cat. You are truly an amazing accountant. You're going places, Mr Blake, keep it up.' He walks a few steps away, then suddenly stops and turns around, wagging his finger in the air.

'Before I forget: Mr Gilberry told me to give this to you.' Mr Hubert places a ring in Jayden's hand and promptly leaves. Jayden notes the engraved letters on top: 'K' and 'O'.

Looking to the ring, then the door, he rushes down to Mr Gilberry's office, knocking on his door very slowly so as not to seem too excited. When he hears Mr Gilberry say 'come in' he makes sure to open the door in a controlled manner.

'Jayden, I'm surprised to see you in my office,' says Mr Gilberry, looking no worse for wear, the epitome of an accountant keeping a cool head in self and appearance.

'Well, when Mr Hubert gave me this,' showing him the ring pinched between his forefinger and thumb, 'I had to see you about it.' He has to make sure that he is being asked to join. 'I thought you said that there were too many incompetent and stupid people here?'

'You are not as stupid as you seem, and incompetence can be cured as long as you are willing to teach the student, and he's willing to learn.'

'I'm more than eager,' Jayden replies. Being Mr Gilberry's ally will get him on a fast track for a promotion in no time.

'Good. I will see you at 5:30 when we can talk more about this. I have work to do that must be finished on time as I refuse to stay late.'

Jayden walks out of the office, but hesitates in the doorway and turns around.

'I just have one more question for you.'

'Yes?'

'Why were you wearing a pink sparkly dress?' Jayden asks curiously.

Mr Gilberry gives him a little smirk.

'Being an accountant and being a Knight of Order is not the only life I have, Mr Blake.'

Beyond The Boundary

Escaping the city, I disappear into the wild green, tracing the path back to the world that's serene.

The sky's hue transforms and the full moon is revealed to me, illuminating the world in its cold gleam. The sea bubbles in warning and I look on in glee, for emerging from the waters is the corpse of Rosa Lee. With silence and guile she walks over to me; her cold clammy hand meets mine and we sit under the old oak tree.

'Are you okay?' I cannot help but say.

'Of course, since you've come my way,' she always conveys.

We roll and prance over the vast green hills. The hours we fill are all thrills. My body sears, my mind is a tizz, and I stumble and spill rolling down the hill. Lying in the still, I cannot help but ask the same question that I always cast.

'Are you sad?'

'Should I be?' asks Rosa Lee.

'Are you mad?'

'Should I be?' asks Rosa Lee.

'Why did you die?' I ask and sigh.

'Accident, no intent, just a misstep into the ferment.'

'Is that a lie?'

'There's only truth in my reply.' The sun tickles my eyes, shining bright, and I see Rosa Lee returning to where it's always night.

'Why can't you be here with me in the day? Why must you go away?' I always say.

'Maybe the moon, maybe the stars, but the answer can't be seen by either you or me; it's only for the gods,' answers Rosa Lee, and returns to the beyond.

I cannot help a moment of sorrow, but I remind myself there is a tomorrow. Now, though, the sun commands the world awake and I must make haste—through the boundary back to crowds, scowls and dead concrete grounds, where the days are long and the people bring me down. I remind myself I will once again bound away from this town.

For the sun will always sleep; the full moon shall once again peak. And when that day comes to be, I shall once again see my Rosa Lee, down by the sea.

Teeth and Fire... A Perfect Smile

Miria jaunts down the sidewalk; numerous fae eyes ghost over the scars that decorate her body. Their diamond gazes turn from sympathy to condescension when they see her pin; in stark contrast, the booksellers and bakers she passes give her small smiles and nods. Their silent encouragement fuels her strenuous journey, and as familiar street names slip by, she can tell that her trek will end in 12 feet and a turn of a corner. Miria's steps falter, but she steadily regains her jaunt, skirting the edge of the building onto Larvell Street, where Varian Complex comes into view.

Her throat goes dry, her body shrieks and her scars ache in kind. Miria shields herself from the view with a mutilated hand. She attempts to trudge ahead, but the pangs and spasms that wrack through each nerve render her helpless, and she's stuck to the pavement. Miria's hand shakily wanders into her pocket. Her fingers grasp her round friend and place the little blue pill between her scarred lips. She swallows the tablet dry and it lands like a stone in her gut. She takes a deep breath and recites her mantra, 'Just put one foot in front of the other.' Her pain slowly subsides and she goes onward, into the towering, majestic beast.

The complex's cold monochrome interior draws her inside, and Miria cautiously takes one step after another across the sea of black tiles till she reaches the bank of the long winding staircase. Miria's foot lifts, and bit by bit her hesitant shoe meets the first beige step and then the next. The rhythmic steady dense thunk on the boards turns to soft taps as she flies up the twisted beige path. A long-forgotten smile emerges on her face.

The vast cityscape rushes beside her and Miria takes in the marvellous view she has missed: the graffitied billboards; the fairies that glide through the air; the roads congested with gaudy carriages. People dash and scuttle about into buildings that tower into the skyline, blocking out any thought of a world outside the bustling metropolis. She could look at the sights till her eyes bleed, but slowly the windows shift up and her view is substituted for white walls.

The stairs disappear underfoot and are replaced by polished black-and-white chequered tiles that lead to the penthouse door. Miria's fingers tingle as she grabs the brass handle and pulls. The entryway wails and cries under her exertion, but relents and opens up into the cluttered space. Her jubilation turns sour at the sight and the door slams behind her.

Books are left stacked out next to the shelves, pens invade every crevice, and assorted designs scribbled on worn paper cover the floor. A sigh breaks through Miria's lips; the once pridefully immaculate room has transformed into disorder during her brief break. Master Avarie desperately needed her back, it seems. All the while, she ignores the little voice in her head that says, 'She kept a spotless space before your arrival.'

Miria sparrows up the old wooden staircase to her Master's residence to start the day, but all she finds is dishes, worn clothes strewn around, and unopened letters piled high on the Civil Sky Rail steps. The room is bursting with her Master's presence, but bare of Master Avarie.

She must be at a dental emergency, Miria concludes, slumping down on a pile of clothes that screeches and throws her to the floor. Miria gets into her stance, primed to fight the sentient fibres, but instead of attacking, her opponent hurls the clothes aimlessly around. The conscious threads diminish to reveal the soft red skin of her Master.

'Master Avarie, there you are! I've been looking all around for you,' Miria says joyfully and bounces over. Her arms stretch around Master Avarie in an anaconda's embrace, but the strong limbs of her Master don't return her embrace and Miria's skin crawls. Her hand edges to her pocket for another pill, but stops; she cannot show her weakness in front of her Master.

'Well, you've found me, unfortunately,' Master Avarie grunts, rubbing the sleep out of her eyes. 'Why are you here? I thought I was picking you up from the hospital.'

Miria's heart beats wild in her chest. 'We're needed at Rivera Casino,' she declares, her chipper tone wavering.

'I need coffee.' Master Avarie pulls herself out of Miria's grasp and heads into the small kitchen. In the sun's illumination Miria sees what Master Avarie hid behind paint and clothes when she visited her. The once-thick, strong horns are flaking; the scales of her tail are turning from their vibrant red to a light pink. She has dark marks under her bright green eyes; her nightclothes hang off her slender, hunched frame. Miria's stomach squeezes, turns, and forms a knot. This is because of her.

'So,' Master Avarie's voice breaks through her thoughts and lands her back into the small room. 'What's the problem this time?' Master Avarie takes a sip of her coffee.

'Sim-Auoil broke another tooth. He bit into a rock on a dare, again.'

'That man never learns. I swear he has a fetish for pain,' says Master Avarie through a mouthful of coffee, and swallows it down. Draining the rest of the cup she looks into the emptiness, as if it holds a secret. She traces the rim with her finger and a sigh escapes her lips.

'Perhaps you should stay here, though... I don't think it's a good idea for you to go there.'

Miria's throat tightens and ears burn at her Master's declaration.

'I'm fine; I can do this,' Miria pleads. The knot in her stomach expands as Master Avarie's brow furrows and her lips thin.

'Miria, as your Master I don't think you are capable...'

'I can, though,' Miria interrupts. 'I need to! Please don't leave me behind. Not when I've done so much to get here. They wouldn't have released me if I wasn't fine.'

Master Avarie's fist softly pecks her own forehead three times. Her tail flicks and she closes her eyes.

'Miria, you're going to be the death of me.' Master Avarie heaves out a long sigh and glances at her wristwatch. 'Get my bag. Get the tools. We leave in five.'

'Yessss!' Miria shouts and races to the top of the staircase, flips over the banister and lands on the papered floor. When she knocks twice on the hardwood of the steps, the door to the lab reveals itself. Miria bounces through the entryway, grabs the big leather bag that hangs on the hook, takes a pair of gloves from the box suspended on the grey-tiled wall, and dons them in front of the autoclave—more out of habit than an actual need to wear them. She releases the pristine tools and places them hygienically into the bag. Shuffling to the left, she opens a drawer and takes out a piece of paper, bandages, disinfectant, gloves and thread; more for show if Master Avarie checks the supplies than for actual use. Miria shuts the mouth of the bag and sets the familiar weight on her shoulders. She peels off her gloves and discards them in the waste bin by the door. She leaves the sanitised area and bounds back up to Master Avarie's bedroom.

'Everything packed?' Master Avarie asks, as she rolls lint off her black top and adjusts the dentistry pin displayed proudly on her chest.

'Yep.'

'Let's get a move on. The Civil Sky Rail won't stick around just for us.' Master Avarie throws the roller on the bed and strides up the stairs with Miria following behind. The mail rustles under her Master's boot, the hatch opens, and in a few steps they arrive at the platform, just as the Civil Sky Rail grinds into view, the sun glinting off its silver exterior. Her chest tightens, and her fingers grow cold. She takes a silent deep breath. The biting cold at her fingers retreats, as well as the vice around her torso.

'We've got great timing,' says Master Avarie with a smile, pressing the button. The doors glide apart and together they cross the threshold into the lone carriage.

'Oh, Master Avarie, I haven't seen you in a while, not since the tribunal,' comes the gentle, familiar voice of Chair Woman Saria from Miria's blind spot. 'It's such a surprise to see you. Tell me—how have you been?'

The doors shut, the carriage buzzes under her heel and continues on its path, trapping Miria in the small, confined space that dangles high above the cityscape. Her Master's tail raises and she slowly turns to Chair Woman Saria. Miria bites her lip; her eyes shift between the two. She needs to kill the conversation before it begins, though her stomach turns at the thought of talking to *her*; but for her Master's sake she will. She plasters a smile on her face that burns her lips.

'Chair Woman Saria, it's wonderful to see you again,' says Miria, interrupting the conversation, and takes the seat opposite her.

'My, my, aren't you a sight for sore eyes, Miria. It's good to see you again, but shouldn't you still be in the hospital?' Saria asks, her cat eyes narrow, furry tail twitching back and forth.

'I just got out today.' Miria glances to the outside world that rushes by, longing for it to start slowing down.

'Oh I see, I see. You're finally headed to the town hall to have your apprenticeship terminated,' goads Chair Woman Saria, igniting a blaze of outrage in her.

'No. I'm assisting Master Avarie at Crown Reveria,' Miria replies sternly. A flush of instant regret washes over her, as the sound of Chair Woman Saria's concerned tutting works its way into her ears.

'Are you sure that's such a good idea?' Chair Woman Saria casts a quizzical eye over Master Avarie, as though Miria couldn't answer for herself.

'I have to go there eventually; it's a part of my job,' Miria pipes in, and regains the full attention of Chair Woman Saria.

'Speaking of jobs, the boutique I frequent is looking for someone to be in back of house,'

Chair Woman Saria kindly tells her. Her innuendo strikes Miria in a brutal assault.

'Errrrr, fashion isn't for me,' Miria forces out through gritted teeth.

'How about a bookstore or a bakery, then? I think a more traditional human role would suit you best.' Chair Woman Saria intrudes into Miria's personal space and pats her shoulder sympathetically, agitating her old burns. 'Dentistry isn't a profession for a human; you simply don't have the constitution for it. I mean, just look what happened to you.' Chair Woman Saria gives a patronising coo that destroys all sense of subtext, as if Miria couldn't see through her words.

Miria clenches her fist at Chair Woman Saria's soft discouragement. How Miria wants to scream about the absolute ignorance and stupidity of her remark! But that won't change the Chair Woman's mind—or the minds of her old teachers, or ex-friends who still hold on to the rhetoric about a human's place in the world—all because of the substandard magic that runs through her veins. Dentistry doesn't even require sorcery—and even if it did, boosting potions exist for that very purpose, though the facts don't matter to someone like Saria; they never did. And if Miria did say something, it would only appear as if she were throwing a tantrum, and she will accomplish nothing except making a fool of herself. So Miria swallows the thorny words that sprout at the back of her mind and remains quiet, staring at her shoes as she's always done in these situations.

'That isn't up to you.'

Hearing her Master's stern voice, Miria's ears become hot and her chest warms.

'True; the matter is no longer in my hands,' Chair Woman Saria shrugs, 'but I cannot help but question your actions. Putting your apprentice through unnecessary mental strain on her first day back, after months of gruelling recovery. Are you sure that's prudent of you, Master Avarie?' Chair Woman Saria rhetorically asks, her warm demeanour shedding to expose her stony inclination. Miria feels the carriage's tumultuous vibrations drop to a hum, the world outside slows and the structures are no longer blurs. 'South March Station' plays on the intercom and the Civil Sky Rail eases to a halt.

'Oh, that's my station. It was nice talking to you, ladies.' Chair Woman Saria strides to the door, presses the button and disembarks.

'Hey, Chair Woman,' Master Avarie calls out and seizes her attention. 'Don't underestimate my apprentice. She survived dragons' breath; and while yours reeks, it's nothing but hot air.' Master Avarie growls, her tail arches over her head and she curtly butts her horns at Chair Woman Saria, who splutters in indignation as the doors close on her shocked vile face, swiftly vanishing from Miria's sight as the view returns to the scenic metropolis.

Master Avarie drops onto the brown plush seat beside Miria. Her posture sags as she stares up at the low ceiling; her eyes glaze over. Miria's insides squirm at the collapsed body of her Master.

'She's wrong.' Miria swings her legs back and forth. 'You're a brilliant teacher; I wouldn't be here if you weren't.' Master Avarie avoids her gaze and her lips once again stretch into thin lines.

'You came close, Miria...' Master Avarie shoulders tremble in a way that leads one to assume it is the carriage that moves her, but Miria can see she's holding back a storm of emotions, and that the wrong word uttered would unleash the tempest that swirls within, '...to not being here,' Master Avarie finishes, leaving words unsaid between them.

'Now arriving at Rivera Casino,' the voice overhead announces, and the Sky Rail comes to a slow stop. Miria's head fills with rushing water;

121

her vision swims; her scars throb, and she discreetly takes another little blue pill. Mechanically she stands up and disembarks onto the barren platform.

The aperture of the casino opens up onto the same view she saw months ago. The bright lights rain down on her and illuminate the white marble path that leads to the impressive golden doors, behind which the muffled sounds of joyful laughter reach out to her, beckoning her inside once again. The knot in her stomach tightens at the incoming hurricane that is about to be unleashed.

'Shouldn't there be...?'

'Helloooooo,' says a Fancy Man, cutting off Master Avarie's sentence halfway.

'Bloody hell!' Master Avarie howls and practically jumps out of her skin at his presence. 'You Fancy Men need to stop popping out of nowhere.'

'I shall rectify my behaviour, ma'am.' He lifts his red, embroidered, bejewelled, bow-and-feather-adorned top hat in customary repentance that, as usual, makes Master Avarie roll her eyes.

'So Sim-Auoil—is he in the blue room or does he want to make a spectacle again in the gambling den?'

The Fancy Man frowns as the hat makes its way back onto his head. The knot in Miria's stomach tightens and explodes under the pressure at the sight of her lie about to be released.

'It seems there's been some miscommunication; the patient is Triures, not Sim-Auoil.' Miria hears her lies unravel with the Fancy Man's sentence, and she waits for the gale that's sure to come. Master Avarie goes quiet, and a chasm of silence stretches between them.

'Miria,' says Master Avarie, bridging the tranquility, her flat tone raising the phantom hairs on Miria's arms.

'Yes?' Miria replies tepidly.

Master Avarie gently removes the bag from her shoulders.

'You stay here,' Master Avarie commands and strikes Miria still, rendering her a spectator to her Master's unwavering strides. As Master Avarie's foot reaches the doorstep, Miria breaks out of the trance.

'No, I'm coming with you.' Miria races after her, but Master Avarie pivots and grabs her by the shoulders in a grip that's sure to bruise.

'No. You're going to stay here while I address this,' Master Avarie snarls.

'I'm your apprentice,' Miria protests. 'I promise I won't fail you again.'

Master Avarie's fingernails dig into Miria's shoulders and, for the first time, she looks Miria in the eye.

'Miria, you didn't. I'm your Master. I'm supposed to protect you and when I saw you on the ground, burnt...' tears drip out of Master

Avarie's eyes and Miria is lost in the unsettlingly foreign expression of dismay that graces her Master's face, '…I thought you were dead and the… and the terror I felt in that moment nearly stopped my heart… I barely got you out, and if I misstep again next time, or if the blast is direct instead of indirect, it will be the…' Master Avarie's voice cracks, and tears cascade down her face. 'I just don't want to lose you,' she whispers.

'I'm sorry,' says Miria breathlessly, and diverts her gaze to the ground. 'When I got the call this morning, I thought to myself, this is my chance to fix my mistakes.' Miria bites her lip and clenches her eyes tight as she struggles to get her confession out. She lifts her head. Her Master's uneasy expression fills her world; her stomach turns. 'I almost turned back when I saw Varian complex because I knew I would come back here, but the moment my foot landed on the beige steps my apprehension flew away. Because there's nothing else I would rather do than be your apprentice and become like you. It's everything to me.' Miria grabs Master Avarie's hands and brings her close. 'I have chosen this, so... so please continue to guide me.'

Master Avarie's gaze drifts to the golden doors and then back to Miria. 'You don't have to do this today; there's always tomorrow,' she whispers.

'I know,' Miria mutters breathlessly, 'but if I don't do this now, I don't think I can continue on as your apprentice.'

Master Avarie rolls her lip between her teeth and her tears slow to a trickle. 'All right, all right.' With quiet reluctance she lets Miria go and hands her back the bag. 'But I won't ever see you burn again.' Master Avarie places her hand on her heart. 'That I vow.'

'Are you ready to go, my ladies?' The Fancy Man asks, reminding Miria of his presence.

'Yes, we are.'

A warm hand slides into Miria's. The Fancy Man ushers them inside from the cold to the rowdy warm interior. He guides them into the bones of the building and down familiar concrete stairs to a steel door where another Fancy Man is waiting with a lantern. The second Fancy Man opens the door with a bow and offers the light to Master Avarie, who takes it. Miria traverses down into the depths, the lantern illuminating nostalgic sights of the vast white cavern. Her scars gnaw into her skin as the stairs become ground, but the warmth of Master Avarie's clasp keeps her hand from reaching for another little blue pill.

'Get ready,' Master Avarie whispers, and Miria takes a deep breath, focusing on the sound of her feet as a large scaly claw comes into view. Then a gigantic scaly green muzzle appears in Miria's sight, and burning, unfocused red eyes. Master Avarie drops Miria's hand and steps forward into the dragon's view.

Master Avarie bows low to the ground. Miria hurries to the side with the bag in hand, and presents it. Sweat drips down her forehead and her heartbeat thumps in her ears, telling her to run, but the little knowledge that burns at the back of her head causes her to stay still. Holding her breath, she waits; the dragon moves its claw and opens its jaws wide. Miria lets out a silent sigh of relief.

Master Avarie climbs into the dragon's mouth, and with her free hand makes a grasping sign. Breaking out of her daze, Miria clumsily opens the bag, sifting through the various tools to find a pair of pliers. She shakily throws them to Master Avarie, who catches them with the tips of her fingers.

Pulling the pliers wide open, she places them around the large rotten tooth nestled among its jagged yellow and white companions. Master Avarie's muscles flex, her teeth clench and her neck strains. Her body heaves and the damaged, putrid tooth is removed. Master Avarie steps forward, but her foot slides back and falls into the cavity.

In a blink, Triures snaps its wide jaws down on Master Avarie. Miria flees. Fire engulfs the cavern and snaps at her heels. Miria's legs shiver and shake as she follows her old tracks behind the white rock that once shielded her. It repeats its role now. She tucks her body in tight; the flames lick around her shaking form, tears drip down her face and her heart jumps into her ears. Her scars ache and she searches her pockets for her pills, but her hands only grasp the lining of her black jacket. They must have fallen out while she was running.

'Miria,' Master Avarie's stern comforting voice cuts through the inferno, almost as if she is right beside her. She can practically see her now: clothes burned away, naked, standing proudly on the dragon's head. What she wouldn't give to be flame-retardant. 'Remember, just wait, strike, and then leap. Don't look in its eyes.'

Master Avarie's words hold her tight in an invisible embrace. Her quivers cease, her tears trickle dry, her heart quietens and the mantra of one foot in front of the other sings in her mind. She turns a nervous eye on the flames and watches their scalding blue transmute to a warm orange that sizzles out. She runs towards the towering form of the dragon. The red eyes meet hers and she sees her end; her legs refuse to move another inch and the tune in her head dies. The dragon opens its jaw and the slumbering embers rouse; now she will burn again.

'Don't you dare make a liar out of me.' Master Avarie's harsh words strike through her terror, and Miria bullets upward, grabbing the dragon's jagged tooth. Her hand reaches out and is met by another; the blaze flares by her soles as she's pulled into Master Avarie's naked, warm, safe grip, the dragon none the wiser to their position on its head. Master Avarie keeps her close, and together they leap off the dragon's back, sneak across the scorched cavern, and climb up the stairs and out of the inferno.

Miria collapses on the stone floor. Sweat flows down her face as she gulps in the air and exhales savagely till her breaths return to their steady pace. She staggers to her feet and Master Avarie's bright vibrant green eyes meet hers. She pats Miria on the head.

'Thank you, Master Avarie.' A grin draws wide on Miria's face and she wraps her arms tight around Master Avarie's naked back. Her Master returns the favour in kind.

About The Author

Eden Van Leeuwen has a passion for writing and has devoted the majority of her life to the craft.

Follow her on Twitter:

https://twitter.com/LeeuwenEden